SILENT INVADERS

BY HARRIETTE S. ABELS

Library of Congress Cataloging in Publication Data

Abels, Harriette Sheffer.
  The silent invaders.
  (Galaxy I)
  SUMMARY: An invading army of humanoids threatens to blow up any
colony whose inhabitants will not vacate.
  (1. Science fiction) I. Title. II. Series.
PZ7.A1595Si   (Fic)   79-4644
ISBN 0-89686-031-0

International Standard Book Numbers:
  0-89686-031-0 Library Bound
  0-89686·040-X Paperback

**Library of Congress
Catalog Card Number:**
79-4644

CRESTWOOD·HOUSE

**P.O. Box 3427
Hwy. 66 South
Mankato, MN 56001**

SILENT
INVADERS
BY HARRIETTE S. ABELS

ILLUSTRATED BY RODNEY
AND BARBARA FURAN

EDITED BY DR. HOWARD SCHROEDER
Professor in Reading and Language Arts
Dept. of Elementary Education
Mankato State University

DESIGNED BY BARBARA FURAN

About the author . . .

Harriette Sheffer Abels was born December 1, 1926 in Port Chester, New York. She attended Furman University, Greenville, South Carolina for one year. In addition to having her poetry published in the Furman literary magazine, she had her first major literary success while at the University. She wrote, produced and directed a three act musical comedy that was a smash hit!

At the age of twenty she moved to California, where she worked as a medical secretary for four years. In September, 1949, she married Robert Hamilton Abels, a manufacturers sales representative.

She began writing professionally in September, 1963. Her first major story was published in **Highlights For Children** in March, 1964, and her second appeared in **Jack and Jill** a short while later. She has been selling stories and articles ever since. Her first book was published by Ginn & Co., for the Magic Circle Program, in 1970.

Harriette and her husband love to travel and are looking forward to their annual trip to Europe. While travel doesn't leave much time for writing, Harriette does try to write at least something every day. When at home a sunporch serves as her office, but she confesses that most of her serious writing is done while stretched out on her bed.

The Abels have three children - Barbara Heidi, David Mark, and Carol Susan, and three dogs - Coco, Bon Bon, and Ginger Ale.

SILENT INVADERS

Emergency Spaceship EM 88 settled easily onto its landing pad. Brita, pilot of the EM 88, leaned back in her chair and stretched.

"That was an easy mission," she said.

"But not very exciting," Joris, her co-pilot, added.

"But delivering emergency rations is important," Brita said.

The intertel in front of Joris buzzed. The voice of Druce, captain of the EM 88, came over the speaker.

"I'm going over to headquarters. Is your flight report ready, Brita? I'll take it with me."

"It's ready, Druce," Brita said. "But I'll go along with you. I want to see the orders for our next mission."

When Brita, Joris and Druce walked into Commander Markey's headquarters, the building was jammed with people.

"What's new in here?" Joris said. "I've never seen so much going on in this place."

Druce went into Commander Markey's office.

"We're back, sir," he said. "What's been going on while we were away?"

Commander Markey sat up behind his desk. "These people are refugees, Druce," he said.

Druce turned and looked back out the office door.

"Refugees from where?" He was puzzled. "Has there been an earthquake? Or a meteor strike?"

"No. It's much more serious than that." Commander Markey looked extremely worried. "These people have come in from our base on Jupiter. They have a very strange story to tell. I'll let you speak to their leader."

Commander Markey went to the door and motioned to a man standing across the room. When he came over, Commander Markey introduced him to Druce.

"This is Varik," the Commander said. "He has been the leader of the Jupiter colony for the past ten years. As you know, we have no permanent colonies on any of the major planets. Only the minor ones, Venus, Mars and Mercury. Varik, tell Druce what happened."

Varik paused. "We aren't exactly sure what happened. We woke up one morning in our base camp and there was a huge army of men surrounding us."

Druce stared at him. "How can that be? Didn't you hear them land? It isn't possible to sneak up on someone in space — especially an undomed colony like yours on Jupiter."

Varik nodded. "That's what I mean. We don't know how they landed. We don't know where they came from. But they ordered us off immediately. There were only several hundred of us. There was no way we could hold out against them. So we got in our spaceships and left."

Druce turned to Commander Markey. "Do you want us to go up and check it out, sir? Is that our mission?"

Commander Markey shook his head. "No, Druce. You haven't heard the whole story yet. While you were out on your last mission, a group came in from the planet Pluto. We have been talking of starting a colony there. This group was sent out to see if this is possible. They were supposed to stay several years. Instead, they returned, telling almost exactly the same story. They awoke one morning and found an invading army had taken over the planet. They were forced to leave."

"But who are these people?" Druce asked. "Is it the same army, the one on Pluto and the one on Jupiter? And how are they sneaking up on everyone?"

Varik said, "It's a complete mystery. None of us can understand how they did it."

"Commander." One of the communicators came running in from the communications room. "Sir. There are several ships asking for permission to land. They are from Asteroid NMA-84."

"NMA-84!" Commander Markey exclaimed. "That's our new asteroid mining operation!"

"Yes, sir," the communicator nodded. "The leader says they've been chased by an invading army."

"What the — !" Commander Markey jumped up. "Druce, contact the other EM captains. I'm going to send a fleet of you to find out what's going on."

"Yes, sir."

Druce went into the communications room and gave orders for all of the EM captains to be contacted immediately. He went out to the main room and explained to Brita and Joris what was going on.

"But that's ridiculous!" Brita exclaimed. "How can invading armies be in all these places at once? Who would have that many men?"

"We don't know," Druce said. "This is the strangest thing I've ever heard."

"Not only strange," Joris said, "it's the most dangerous."

"Druce!" Captain Markey called to him from his office. "Get in here immediately!"

"We've just had an emergency call from Asteroid NMA-6. They have been threatened with invasion from a fleet of spaceships. They said the asteroid is surrounded with them."

"NMA-6!" Druce said. "That's Orel's mining operation."

"That's right," Commander Markey said. "Orel told the invaders that they had no way to leave the asteroid. They have been ordered to get it immediately from us."

"We'll leave as soon as the EM 88 is ready, sir."

Druce hurried back to get Brita and Joris, then they raced out to the spaceship.

"Get the crew together," Druce said. "Tell them we take off at 1100 hours."

After takeoff, EM 88 sped quickly through space toward NMA-6. They docked on the mining asteroid and found Orel and her mining crew waiting to be taken off.

Druce looked around. "Has the invading army landed?" he asked.

Orel shook her head. "No. The spaceships left as soon as we told them you were coming. But they warned us if we weren't gone by tomorrow, they would invade."

Druce looked thoughtful. "That's very interesting," he said. "I wonder why they left." He stared into space. "And where did they go? Are they out there watching us?" He turned to Orel. "Are you willing to take a chance?"

"On what?" Orel asked.

"Stay here until tomorrow." He pointed toward the EM 88. "We'll stay with you. Let's see what happens when they find you are still here in the morning."

Orel thought for a moment. "All right," she said. "We'll stay if the workers agree."

She put the question to them. Some of the workers wanted to leave immediately. But it was finally decided that they would be safe with the EM 88 ready to take off in a hurry if necessary.

"Shall we sleep in the spaceship tonight?" Orel asked.

"No," Druce said. "We'll bunk in the living quarters, just as we always do. We know we're leaving tomorrow. But I want them to wonder what we're doing."

There was little conversation at the evening meal. The crew of the EM 88 and the mine workers all waited nervously to see what would happen next. They went to bed early.

Druce said good night to Orel. "Call me the moment they communicate with you in the morning if I'm not already awake."

"Of course," Orel agreed. "And Druce, we will be leaving anyhow."

"Don't worry," he said. "We'll be out of here by 1200 hours tomorrow."

Druce slept soundly, awakening at 0600. As he walked in for the morning meal, he saw that most of the others were awake and dressed, too. Orel was seated at a corner table. Druce joined her.

"No word yet?" he asked.

She shook her head. "Nothing."

Suddenly Zelig, one of the workers, shouted, "Orel, come quickly! Look!"

Orel and Druce ran to the window where Zelig was standing. Druce could hardly believe his eyes as he stared out at the gray rocky surface of the asteroid. A large army of men covered every inch of the bare rock.

"Where did they come from?" Druce whispered. "I know they weren't there five minutes ago."

"And how did they get there?" Orel asked. "No one heard anything."

"Where's your communicator?" Druce asked.

"Over in the office building," Orel said. "Oh! I hope nothing has happened to her!"

Druce started for the door.

"Wait," Orel called. "Remember. You must wear a spacesuit out there."

"I almost forgot," Druce said.

Quickly, he grabbed a suit and went outside.

"Who are you?" he called. "What do you want?"

A loud voice boomed back at him. "This asteroid was supposed to be vacated," the voice said. "Why have you not followed our instructions?"

Druce felt a terrible fear. Although the army was several hundred yards away from him, there was a strange, unearthly look to them. The men stared straight ahead. He couldn't tell which one was speaking.

"You are to leave now," the voice ordered. "We will not wait a moment longer."

Druce turned and hurried back into the building.

"We'd better do as they say," he said. "They outnumber us tremendously. We have no chance against them. Quick! Everyone. Into your spacesuits. Run to the EM 88. We'll take off immediately."

Within minutes, the living quarters was clear. The crew and the mine workers boarded the EM 88 and Brita took the ship off the landing pad and into space as quickly as possible.

Back at the headquarters Astro-lab, Druce reported in to Commander Markey.

"I've never seen anything like it." He was puzzled. "They appeared out of nowhere."

"What did they come in?" Commander Markey asked.

"I don't know," Druce said. "It all happened so

fast. I didn't see spaceships. I didn't see anything."

"Were they humanoids?"

"Oh, yes," Druce said. "In fact, they looked no different than we earthlings. We — " He suddenly stopped. "Commander!" he exclaimed. "I hadn't realized until this minute. That army was standing on the bare asteroid without spacesuits!"

The commander slumped in his chair. "They were able to survive in open space?" He sounded as if he couldn't believe what he was hearing. "Then they are not of our galaxy," he said. "They are not earthlings."

Druce thought for a moment. "No, but they are humanoids."

"We've had several calls since you left for NMA-6," Commander Markey said. "We've sent other ships for rescue mission. So far, no one else has seen an army."

Druce hung his head. "I'm afraid that was my fault, sir. If we had taken the miners off yesterday, as we were told to, we wouldn't have seen them either."

"There has been a threat against the Mercury colony," the commander said. "I'm sending you to get them."

"Yes, sir," Druce said. "And this time we won't hang around."

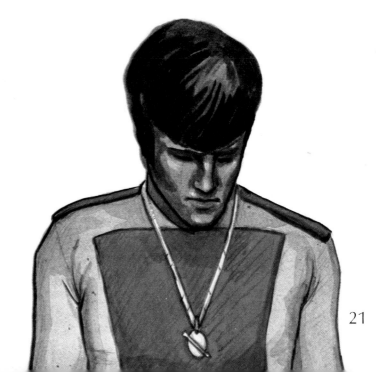

"Just a moment." The commander held up his hand. He stared right into Druce's eyes. "I want you to hang around. I want you to observe everything about them that you can. I'm going to send Curran with you."

"Curran!" Druce said. "Isn't he a scientist of some kind?"

"He's an anthropologist," Captain Markey said. "I want to see if he can identify these people."

As soon as Curran was located and briefed on the mission, the EM 88 crew prepared for takeoff. Within hours, they were on their way to the Mercury colony.

When they landed, Druce explained the plan to the leader of the colony. "Nothing can happen," Druce assured him. "We will have everything ready for emergency boarding. But we must pretend for now that we are not leaving the colony."

"But how can you be sure — ?" the leader began.

"We can't," Druce said. "But so far, no one has been hurt in any way. Whoever these people are, they threaten a lot, but they haven't done anything."

Druce returned to his cabin aboard the EM 88. He pushed a lever on his intertel.

"Rina," he said. "Come down here at once."

In a few minutes, the navigator of the EM 88 walked into his office.

"What is it, Druce?" she asked.

"You know why we're here," Druce began.

"Yes," Rina said. "I was at the briefing."

"Commander Markey sent Curran with us because he's an anthropologist. He's hoping he will be able to identify these people."

Druce stood up and came around his desk. He stood next to Rina.

"But I think you can be of even more help."

Rina smiled. "You mean with my supersight."

"Exactly," Druce said. "We will all be observing them closely. That is, if they show themselves again. But you will be able to see things that we won't. On the asteroid, they didn't come close enough for me to see them clearly. They were just a blur of bodies."

"I understand," Rina said. "I'll try and remember everything I see."

Everything was quiet in the planet colony that evening.

The following morning, when they got up, it was exactly the same as it had been on the mining asteriod, out of nowhere, a huge army was gathered inside at one end of the dome.

The leader of the colony was scared. "Where did they come from?" he gasped. "How did they get inside the dome?"

"That's what we can't figure out," Druce told him. "And that's why Commander Markey wanted us to stay until they got here. I know this is a frightening experience. But remember, so far they have not hurt anyone. Try to observe everything about them that you can."

Once again, a voice boomed out from the armed mass of men. It was the same voice Druce heard on the asteroid.

"Did you not receive our instructions?" the voice asked. "You are to leave this planet immediately. Do as we say or we will see to it that you leave."

Druce took a few steps forward. He still could not make out where the voice was coming from.

"We will not leave this planet," he said. "Who are you? What right do you have to be here?"

"Do not ask questions," the voice boomed. "Do as you are told. Leave immediately."

"And what will you do if we don't leave?" Druce asked.

For a moment, there was silence. Then the voice could be heard again.

"Look around you," it said. "Look up into the dome."

Druce's head jerked up. Outside, flying around and around the dome, was a huge fleet of spaceships. They did not try to land. They merely kept circling the dome.

"Druce, I can't believe it," Brita said. She was standing next to him. "There are hundreds of them. Hundreds."

"Where are they from?" Druce asked. "Can you tell?"

"No." She shook her head. "I've never seen that symbol before."

"We'd better do as they ask," Druce said.

He found the leader of the colony. "Get your people on board the EM 88," he said. "We'll take you back to headquarters."

Curran was standing off to one side. He was busy making notes.

"Do you recognize them?" Druce asked.

Curran looked up. "Yes." His face was grim. "They are the Ingtars. We have had trouble with them before."

A voice suddenly boomed across the colony again.

"If you are not gone within one hour," the voice said, "we shall blow up this colony."

"Blow up!" Brita gasped. "But there are no explosives allowed in space!"

"These people don't pay attention to rules," Curran said grimly. "The Ingtars are a menace in space. They are — "

"Where are they from?" Brita asked.

"Zeta galaxy," Curran said. "But they've been thrown out of there too. We don't know where their colony is now."

"It must be a huge colony," Druce said, "if this is just their army."

"We'd better get back on board," Curran said. "I don't trust them. They're likely to do exactly what they say."

"You mean they would really blow up a colony?" Druce asked.

Curran nodded. "They once destroyed an asteroid that they wanted to mine. When we protested, they blew it up."

"I never heard about that," Druce said.

"Oh, that was hundreds of years ago," Curran said. "In fact, we were hoping that they had disappeared or returned to Zeta galaxy. We study about

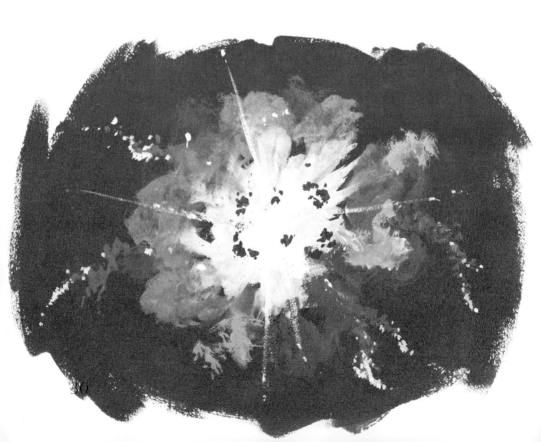

them when we're learning about the different peoples of the universe."

"They look exactly like we do," Joris commented.

"Yes," Curran nodded. "We think they are from a planet in Zeta that matches Earth. We believe they have evolved in the same way that man did."

When they were back in the EM 88, Brita took the ship up as soon as everything was in place.

Druce called a meeting in his cabin. Rina, Curran and Joris were there.

"All right," Druce said when everyone was seated. "I want to know exactly what you saw. Curran, we'll start with you. Identify them again for everyone."

Curran repeated what he had told Druce about the Ingtars.

"There's no question that that's who they are?" Joris said.

"I'm sure of it," Curran answered.

"Rina, what did you see?" Druce asked.

Rina looked at Druce for a long moment. "I'm not sure what I saw," she said. "I saw an army of men. They looked like humans. But there was something strange."

"In what way?" Druce asked.

Rina shook her head. "I don't know. I'm not

sure what was wrong." She slapped her hand on the desk. "But something was wrong. There was something odd about that army."

Druce gave a little smile. "Yes. That was my feeling when I saw them on the asteroid."

"Well," Rina asked, "what was it?"

Druce shook his head. "I don't know. I can't figure it out, either. Could you tell which one of them was speaking?"

"No." Rina made a face. "That's another strange thing. Their mouths were moving, but I couldn't hear what they were saying. Maybe they were too far away." She laughed, "I have supersight. I don't have superhearing."

"There was no noise from that army," Curran said. "If they were speaking, they were whispering."

"That was my feeling," Joris said. "In fact, I thought they were very quiet for an invading army."

"And what about that fleet of spaceships?" Druce asked. "Where did they come from, all of a sudden like that? One minute there was nothing in space. The next it was filled with a fleet of ships."

"There's something strange about this whole thing," Rina said. She stood up. "I'm going back to my cabin. I want to do some thinking about this."

"Yes." Curran jumped up, too. "Now that I know who they are, I am going to do some research."

"Very well," Druce said. "But I expect you all to meet with me in Commander Markey's office as soon as we land."

When the refugees from the planet colony had gotten off the ship, Druce and the others reported immediately to Commander Markey. They told him everything they had seen.

"What next?" Commander Markey asked.

"I'd like another look at them," Curran said.

"Yes," Rina agreed. "I would too. I'm beginning to suspect something."

"About what?" Commander Markey asked.

Rina shook her head. "I don't want to say anything until I'm sure."

"Next time I'll send another spaceship with you," Commander Markey said.

"If I'm right," Rina said, "we won't need them, sir. There isn't any danger at all."

"What do you mean, there isn't any danger?" Commander Markey said. "They've chased a half a dozen colonies — they've threatened to blow up Mercury. Curran says they're the Ingtars, and we know from history that they did at one time blow up an asteroid. How can you say there isn't any danger?"

"I can't say for sure, sir," Rina said. "But if what I suspect is true. . .never mind. We'll see on the next mission."

A new threat came the following day.

"It's the Mars colony this time," Commander Markey said when Druce reported to his office. "And in spite of what your navigator said, please be careful."

"Yes, sir," Druce said. "We'll try the same routine again."

The Mars leader was willing to wait to leave when Druce explained all that had happened before.

The following morning, when Druce walked outside, once again an army was gathered at the end of the planet colony. The same voice boomed into the air.

"Why are you not leaving?" the voice asked. "You are making us angry. We have told you to leave."

Rina stood behind Druce. "Keep him talking," she whispered. "And don't pay any attention to what I do."

"We do not plan to leave," Druce said, exactly as he had said on Mercury.

The voice answered him in the same way. "If you do not leave at once, we shall blow up this planet. We are taking over." The voice roared on.

Druce could see from the corner of his eye that Rina was moving slowly and quietly toward the army. A feeling of panic rushed through him. He spun around to Joris.

"What is she doing?" he whispered loudly. "She's crazy!"

Joris shook his head. "Leave her alone," he said. "She seems to have this figured out."

"But they'll kill her if she gets too close."

"Druce, give her a chance," Joris said. "She seems very sure of what she is doing."

Druce turned to Curran. "Do you see anything new?" he asked.

"No." Curran shook his head. "They're Ingtars. They're dressed as they were the last time. And they just seem to be standing there."

"She's almost there, Druce," Brita said in a low voice. "How are we going to save her if they grab her?"

Druce didn't know what to do. "I'm going to send someone to get her," he said finally.

"Wait!" Joris grabbed his arm. "She's coming back."

Rina came hurrying toward them.

The voice boomed once again. "If you do not leave immediately, we shall attack. Look up into the dome."

Again they looked up to find the fleet of space-ships circling the dome.

"We have to get out of here," Druce said to Rina.

She laughed out loud. "No you don't. No one's going to do a thing to anyone."

"How can you say that?" Druce asked. "An enormous army is stationed at one end of the colony. A fleet of a hundred or more spaceships is circling outside. And you say that we have nothing to worry about?"

"Come with me." Rina motioned to them. She began to walk back toward the army.

"Rina, stop!" Druce ordered.

"Come with me," she insisted. "You'll see. There's nothing to worry about."

Slowly Druce, Curran and Joris followed her across the domed colony toward the army. The figures in the army grew clearer with every step. When they were a few hundred meters away, Rina stopped. The others stood behind her.

"Now watch this," she said, laughing.

She suddenly ran right into the middle of the army.

"Rina!" Druce yelled. "What are you doing?"

Curran gasped. "But, but — " he stuttered. "Look. She's right in the middle of the — and — and — nothing!"

Druce stared wildly. "Nothing's happening!" he said. "They're ignoring her!"

Rina turned around and came back. "Of course they're ignoring me," she said. "They aren't even there!"

"What are you talking about?" Druce shook her gently. "What is going on?"

"There's nobody there." Rina turned around and made a big sweeping motion with her arm. "There's nothing there but some kind of image projection."

"What?" Joris stepped forward. He moved carefully into the crowd of invading Ingtars. When he was in the middle of the army, he turned and faced Druce and the others. He was laughing, too.

"She's right," he cried. "There's nothing here. Look." He swung his arms around, and Druce could see that they passed right through the bodies of the so-called army.

"But I don't understand," Druce said. "Where is it coming from?"

Rina looked up. "Probably from a spaceship out there somewhere. And by the way, I don't think that fleet of ships circling around up there is real, either. I think it's just another image projection."

The voice suddenly boomed again. "Your time is growing short. You are about to be blown off the planet."

"We have to do something about him," Druce said. "Do you think he's here on the planet?"

"Of course he's not here," Rina said. "That's coming from space, too. There's probably one small spaceship someplace equipped with an image projectory and a voice projector. There's no army at all."

"You're right," Druce said. "If there were a real army, they wouldn't have to use an imaginary one."

"Exactly," Curran said. "Maybe we've been right all along. Maybe the Ingtars are practically extinct."

"Or maybe they've been thrown off another planet in their own galaxy," Druce said. "And they're looking for a new place to settle."

"Then why have they been threatening so many of our colonies?"

"Knowing the Ingtars," Curran said, "they're probably just being mean. They got away with the image projection the first time and decided to keep on using it."

"Come on," Druce said. "We'd better get back to the ship. Commander Markey has to hear about this."

Druce assured the leader of the Mars colony that there was no reason for them to leave the planet. He explained as quickly as he could what was going on.

"Don't worry if you can still see the army," he said. "They aren't really there at all. Just go on about your business."

By the time the EM 88 was back at headquarters Astro-orb, the Ingtars had been found and captured.

"It was easy," Commander Markey said, "once we knew what we were looking for. They were hiding on a deserted mining asteroid. They had a whole setup there." He turned to Rina. "How did you know it was image projection and not a real army?" he asked.

"When I saw them the second time," Rina said, "I was sure of it. The first time, I knew there was something strange. You know, a three-dimensional picture does not look exactly like a real object. The second time I saw them, I realized I was looking at the same faces. They were standing in exactly the same place. Their mouths were moving the same way they had the first time. I realized that what I was seeing was the same picture being run again and again. I was sure of it when the spaceship came over. They were flying in the same formation as the first time, with the same distances between them all. That would have been impossible to duplicate."

"Rina," Commander Markey said, "your super-sight has been useful many times. But this time was the best of all. You saved us from an invading army."

Rina and Druce started to laugh.

"Yes," Druce said. "But it was an army that didn't exist!"